Ms. Joni Is a Phony!

Dan Gutman

Pictures by
Jim Paillot

SCHOLASTIC INC.

To Toby Katz

ISBN 978-1-338-18965-0

Text copyright © 2017 by Dan Gutman. Illustrations copyright © 2017 by Jim Paillot.
All rights reserved. Published by Scholastic Inc., 557 Broadway, New York, NY 10012,
by arrangement with HarperCollins Children's Books, a division of
HarperCollins Publishers. SCHOLASTIC and associated logos are
trademarks and/or registered trademarks of Scholastic Inc.

12 11 10 9 8 7 6 5 4   17 18 19 20 21 22

Printed in the U.S.A.   40

First Scholastic printing, May 2017

Typography by Kathleen Duncan

Contents

Zombie-Free Zone

My name is A.J. and I hate zombies.

Zombies are dead people who come back to life. That's weird.

I've never seen a zombie in the real world. But after I go to sleep, my dad watches this TV show about zombies, and one night I sneaked over to the top of the stairs to watch. It was scary!

After that I was sure there was a family of zombies living in my bedroom closet. I told my dad, and he got out the vacuum cleaner and used it to suck up all the zombies that were living in my closet. It was like *Ghostbusters*. But I'm not going to use my closet anymore, just to be on the safe side. And I'm *never* going to use the vacuum cleaner, because there's a family of zombies living inside it.

Don't worry. There's nothing else about zombies in this book. Don't you hate it when you're reading a book and they start talking about stuff that has nothing to do with the book?*

Anyway, it was Friday, my third favorite

---

*Ha-ha, made you look! The story is up there, dumbhead!

day of the week. Why is Friday my third favorite day of the week? Because on Friday, there's no school tomorrow!

My teacher, Mr. Cooper, came flying into the room. Mr. Cooper thinks he's a superhero. But he's not a very good one, because he slipped on a sheet of paper and almost slammed his head into the cloakroom door. Mr. Cooper was carrying

an armful of papers, and they scattered all over the place when he fell.

"Guess what?" Mr. Cooper asked.

"Your butt?" said Michael, who never ties his shoes.

"You ate a cashew nut?" said Ryan, who will eat anything, even stuff that isn't food.

"You got a crew cut?" said Alexia, this girl who rides a skateboard all the time.

"You went to Pizza Hut?" said Neil, who we call the nude kid even though he wears clothes.

Any time somebody asks "Guess what?" you should always answer with obnoxious rhymes. That's the first rule of being a kid.

"No," said Mr. Cooper. "Monday will be Picture Day! Everybody take one of these forms and bring it home to your mom or dad to fill out."

"*Eeek!* Picture Day?" yelled Andrea Young, this annoying girl with curly brown hair. "I *love* Picture Day!"

"Me too!" said Emily, who always loves everything that Andrea loves.

"We have to draw pictures?" I asked. "What's the big deal? We draw pictures all the time."

"No, dumbhead!" Andrea told me, rolling her eyes. "Picture Day is when a photographer comes to school and takes our picture for the yearbook."

I was going to say something mean to

Andrea, but she and the girls were jumping up and down and freaking out about Picture Day.

"What are you going to wear?"

"What are you going to wear?"

"What are you going to wear?"

In case you were wondering, all the girls were asking what they were going to wear.

Ugh. Girls are always worried about what they're going to wear. If you're a girl and you're reading this, let me give you a clue—nobody cares what you wear! You could all wear laundry bags over your heads and I wouldn't notice.

Come to think of it, it would be cool if

all the girls came to school wearing laundry bags over their heads.

"I'm going to wear my new blue dress!" said Andrea.

"I'm going to wear *my* new blue dress too," said Emily, who always does everything Andrea does.

Ugh. I'm going to wear whatever is on the top of my drawer.

"I'm going to wear my new shades," said Ryan.

"Why would you take the shades off your windows?" I asked.

It would be weird to wear window shades.

"Not *those* kinds of shades, dumbhead!" said Ryan. "Shades are sunglasses."

"Oh, I knew that," I lied. "Why are you going to wear shades on Picture Day?"

"Because shades look cool," Ryan told me. "Secret agents always wear shades. I want to look like a secret agent in the yearbook."

Ryan is weird.

I hate Picture Day. Do you want to know the thing I hate the *most* about Picture Day?

I'm not going to tell you.

Okay, okay, I'll tell you.

But you have to read the next chapter. So nah-nah-nah boo-boo on you.*

---

*Hey, how come this book is called *Ms. Joni Is a Phony!* when there's no character named Ms. Joni?

The Torture Department

The thing I hate most about Picture Day is that my mom forces me to buy new clothes. Ugh, I hate shopping! And the worst kind of shopping is clothes shopping, because you have to spend hours trying on clothes.

I don't mind grocery shopping so much.

You don't have to try stuff on at the super-market. Like, you don't have to try on the bananas before you buy them. That would be weird.

"Let's *go*, A.J.!" my mom shouted up the stairs on Saturday morning. "We have to get you new clothes for Picture Day."

"What's wrong with my old clothes?" I hollered back.

"You'll have the picture for the rest of your life," my mom said. "That way you'll know what you looked like when you were in third grade. Don't you want to look nice for the picture?"

"No."

It isn't fair! I thought only the *girls* had

to care about looking nice. Boys should be allowed to look like slobs. That's the first rule of being a boy.

I could have begged and pleaded and cried and freaked out. Sometimes that works. But I knew there was no arguing with my mom. When your mom wants to go shopping, there's no stopping her. That's the first rule of being a mom.

We drove a million hundred miles to the department store. A department store is a store that has a lot of departments, so it has the perfect name.

My mom got a shopping cart. You know it's bad news when your mom gets a shopping cart, because that means she's planning to be shopping for a *long* time. Ugh. But shopping carts are cool, too, because it's fun to run around the department store pushing a cart and bumping into stuff.

We wheeled our cart past the furniture department.

We wheeled our cart past the kitchen department.

We wheeled our cart past the garden department.

Man, department stores have a *lot* of departments.

Finally, we got to the boys' department. Or as I call it, THE TORTURE DEPARTMENT. And you'll never believe what was in the boys' department.

Boys!

Well, of *course* there were boys in the boys' department. That's why it's called the boys' department! But the boys in the boys' department weren't just *any* boys. They were my friends Michael, Ryan, and Neil!

"What are *you* guys doing here?" I asked.

"The same thing *you're* doing here," grumbled Michael.

"We have to buy new clothes for Picture Day," grumbled Ryan.

"Bummer in the summer," grumbled Neil.

The guys were all with their mothers. None of our dads were there. I can't wait until I'm a dad so I won't have to go clothes shopping anymore.

Actually, my mom wanted my dad to come, but he said he would rather poke hot needles in his eyes than go clothes shopping. That was weird. I don't know why anybody would want to poke hot needles in their eyes.

Our moms were all gabbing about the weather and other boring stuff that grown-ups talk about. That's when this salesman came over. His name tag said "Mr. Bob."

"What can I do for you young men?" Mr. Bob asked us.

"You can close the store early so we can get out of here," I told him.

"Very funny, A.J.," said my mom. "Mr. Bob, these boys need new clothes for Picture Day."

"Aha! Picture Day! You boys came to the right place," said Mr. Bob. "What are your favorite colors?"

"Yellow," said Ryan and Neil.

"Plaid," said Michael.

"Orange," I said.

"These boys need plain dark pants, white shirts, dark jackets, and ties," said Ryan's mom.

Ties? Really? I *hate* ties! What's the deal with ties? Ties are dumb. The last time I wore a tie, I thought I was gonna choke.

17

Mr. Bob led us to a rack of boring-looking man clothes for boys. Then we had to go in the fitting room to try them on.

The fitting room is the only good thing about the torture department. They have a mirror in there that lets you see yourself from three sides, all at the same time. That is *cool*. And it's even cooler when you stick your face right next to the line where two mirrors meet.

"Hey look," I told the guys. "I have one eye in the middle of my head!"

We spent a million hundred hours trying on clothes. I thought I was gonna die. Mr. Bob had to keep running back and forth getting other clothes because our moms were never satisfied. Poor Mr. Bob. I can't believe he has to work in the torture department every day. Mr. Bob should get a medal, or a new job.

"Are you kids almost done in there?" shouted Michael's mom.

Finally, we all had on our new suits. Mr. Bob helped us tie our ties. We looked just like our dads, but shorter. So naturally, we had to play a game I call Pretend to Be Your Dad.

"Look, I'm Mr. Businessman," I told the guys as we looked in the mirror. "Give me your money."

"You're fired!" said Ryan. "Let's read the newspaper and go play golf."

"Nice weather we're having," said Michael. "I need some coffee."

"I'm a funeral director," said Neil. "After we bury the bodies, let's go watch the game."

Our moms were calling us, so we had to stop playing Pretend to Be Your Dad and come out of the fitting room. Mr. Bob lined us up, just like they do at the police station with bank robbers.

That's when the weirdest thing in the history of the world happened. Our moms burst out crying.

"Aren't they handsome?" blubbered my mom.

"They look so grown up!" blubbered Michael's mom.

Sheesh, get a grip! The moms were

sobbing and slobbering all over the place. They started pulling tissues out of their purses and blowing their noses into them.

Well, they were blowing their noses into the *tissues*, not into their purses. It would be weird to blow your nose into a purse.

"I can't believe my baby Ryan looks so mature and grown-up," said Ryan's mom. "It seems like only yesterday that he was wearing diapers."

"You were wearing diapers yesterday?" I asked Ryan.

The moms took out their cell phones and started taking pictures of us. Do you know what a bunch of moms are called when they take pictures of you?

Mamarazzi! Get it?*

"Say 'cheese'!" my mom shouted.

Ugh. Why do you have to say "cheese" every time somebody takes your picture? What does cheese have to do with pictures? I don't even like cheese.

"Stop scowling, boys," said Mr. Bob. "Smile for the camera."

"You look *very* handsome, A.J.!" said my mom.

"I look terrible," I replied. "I hate getting my picture taken."

"Don't mind my son," Mom told Mr. Bob. "He *says* he hates everything."

"I understand," Mr. Bob replied. "I was a boy once."

---

*Mamarazzi? Paparazzi? That's what you call a joke!

"Just once?" I said. "I'm a boy *all* the time."

Mr. Bob is a nut job.

The mamarazzi took pictures of us from every possible angle. After a while, my face hurt from smiling.

Finally, we were finished in the torture department. My mom paid for the suit, and I pushed our shopping cart out to the parking lot. That's when I got the greatest idea in the history of the world.

"Hey Mom," I said. "Since you took all those pictures of me in my new suit, we don't need to take any pictures on Picture Day. So, can I stay home from school on Monday?"

"No!"

Picture Day

It was Monday. Picture Day. The worst day in the history of the world.

I know I said there aren't any zombies in this book, but did you ever hear about the Picture Day Zombie? My friend Billy, who lives around the corner, told me about it. The Picture Day Zombie is a zombie who only comes out on Picture Day, so he has the perfect name. If you ask me, that's just something Billy made up to scare people.

Don't worry, there won't be anything else about zombies for the rest of this book. I promise.

Anyway, I got dressed. My new jacket was really uncomfortable. My tie was cutting into my neck. I thought I was gonna die. My parents were in the kitchen drinking coffee and reading the newspaper, because that's what parents have to do. It's the law.

Before I could leave for school, they had to fill out the sheet of paper Mr. Cooper had given us. It was an order form so we could buy pictures.

"Package #1 is two eight-by-tens and two five-by-sevens," my mom told my dad. "Package #2 is three eight-by-tens and four five-by-sevens. And Package #3 is five eight-by-tens and six five-by-sevens. Which package should we buy, dear?"

"I couldn't care less," Dad replied.

My dad and me are a lot alike.

"The important thing, A.J.," he told me, "is to turn in this envelope and make sure you don't lose it. Money doesn't grow on trees, you know."

"Actually, it *does*," I told him. "Money is made out of paper, right? And paper is made out of trees. So money *does* grow on trees."

"Go to school now," said my dad.

Arguing with your parents is fun. That's the first rule of being a kid.

I took the envelope full of money and put it in my backpack. When I got to school, everybody was dressed up in their new Picture Day clothes.

"You look *very* handsome, Arlo!" said annoying Andrea, who calls me by my real name because she knows I don't like it.

"I do *not*," I told her.

"Ooooo!" Ryan said. "Andrea said A.J. looks handsome. They must be in *love*!"

"When are you gonna get married?" asked Michael.

Andrea had one of those rolling suit-cases with her. She opened it, and it was filled with mirrors, combs, hair spray, and all kinds of other junk girls use. Man, it sure takes a lot of stuff to make Andrea look good.

She started fussing with her hair. That's when the most amazing thing in the history of the world happened.

Emily walked into the room.

Well, that's not the amazing part. Emily walks into the room every day. The amazing part was that she was wearing a ski mask over her face!

There are only two reasons why you would wear a ski mask. The first reason is because you're going skiing. The second reason is that you're going to rob a bank. Bank robbers always wear ski masks. I guess they like to go skiing after they

finish robbing a bank.

I knew Emily wasn't going skiing, and I was pretty sure she wasn't going to rob a bank either.

Everybody was looking at her.

"Don't look at me!" she shouted.

"What's wrong, Emily?" asked Mr. Cooper. "Are you okay?"

"I have . . . a pimple!"

Oh. I guess there are *three* reasons why you would wear a ski mask.

Emily started crying, as usual. She took off the ski mask. Her pimple was *tiny*. Nobody ever would have noticed it if she hadn't been wearing a ski mask. And I never would have looked at her if she hadn't told us not to look at her.

Emily is weird.

"Don't worry, Emily," Mr. Cooper told her. "That won't show up in your picture. They can Photoshop that pimple right off your face."

Emily stopped crying. We pledged the allegiance, and then an announcement came over the loudspeaker.

"All classes, please report to the play-ground."

"They're going to shoot the photo of the whole school!" said Andrea. "I'm so excited!"

We had to walk a million hundred miles to the playground. There were bleachers out there, and most of the classes were already on them. Our school has about five hundred kids.

Our class lined up across the back row of the bleachers. Ryan, Michael, and Neil were all the way on the right side. I had to stand between Emily and Andrea on the left side. Ugh.

Everybody was talking. Our principal, Mr. Klutz, came out. He has no hair at all. If we used hair instead of money, he would be broke. Mr. Klutz held up his hand and made a peace sign, which means "shut up." So we all stopped talking.

He told us that the photographer's name was Ms. Joni and that she would be here any minute.

That's when the most amazing thing in

the history of the world happened. There was a noise in the sky.

We all looked up.

A helicopter was flying around.

It was getting lower.

Then it landed in the middle of the playground!

And you'll never believe who got out of the helicopter.

No, I'm not going to make you wait until the next chapter to find out. I'll tell you right now.

It was Ms. Joni!*

---

*It's about time she showed up!

Two Heads Are Better Than One

Ms. Joni was really tall and skinny. She went over and hugged Mr. Klutz like they were old friends.

"Ms. Joni and I are old friends," Mr. Klutz told us. "We went to college together, and then she went on to become a famous photographer. Her pictures are in all the fashion magazines. It was so nice of her to come here to take pictures of you kids for Picture Day."

We gave Ms. Joni a standing ovation. It *had* to be a standing ovation, because we were all standing.

"Well, hello and thank you!" Ms. Joni said. "It is simply *fabulous* to be here. You all look *fabu-lous*. And this is a *fabulous* school. I bet my old friend Mr. Klutz is a *fabulous* principal."

Man, Ms. Joni sure says "fabulous" a lot. Just about every other word from her mouth was "fabulous."

"Blah blah fabulous blah blah fabulous blah blah fabulous blah blah fabulous blah blah," said Ms. Joni.

See what I mean?

"Ms. Joni is really *famous*!" Andrea whispered in my ear. "She takes pictures of all the supermodels."

"Models have superpowers?" I said. "That is *cool*."

I wondered which superpowers models have. It would be cool to have superheat vision. Then you wouldn't need a micro-wave oven. You could just heat up your food by looking at it.

"Supermodels don't have superpowers, dumbhead!" Andrea told me. "They're the most famous models in the world."

"I knew that," I lied.

What is Andrea's problem? Why can't a truck full of microwave ovens fall on her head?

"I bet *you* could be a supermodel, Andrea," whispered Emily.

"People *do* tell me I have nice cheek-bones," Andrea whispered back.

Cheekbones? What?! Cheeks have bones? That's a new one on me. I felt my cheeks. They were all skin. I don't have bones in my cheeks. How would you be able to eat if you had bones in your cheeks? Gross! The whole idea of cheekbones made me want to throw up.

Ms. Joni set up a big camera on a tripod. She told us it was a special camera that would slowly move from left to right as it was taking the picture so it could get all five hundred of us in the shot. We would have to stay perfectly still for five seconds while the camera moved across all our faces.

"Okay," said Ms. Joni. "When I say 'smile,' everybody stay still for five seconds. Ready?"

"Ready!" we all said.

That's when I got the greatest idea in

the history of the world.

"Smile!" said Ms. Joni.

The camera was pointing at my side of the bleachers. As soon as it started moving, I jumped down off the back of the bleachers.

"One . . . ," said Ms. Joni.

I landed on the grass behind the right bleachers.

"Two . . . ," said Ms. Joni.

I ran across the back of the bleachers to the other side, where my friends were.

"Three . . . ," said Ms. Joni.

I climbed up the back of the bleachers.

"Four . . . ," said Ms. Joni.

I stood up between Ryan and Michael.

"Five . . . ," said Ms. Joni.

The camera was pointing right at my side of the bleachers.

"Fabulous!" said Ms. Joni. "Nice job standing still, everybody."

"A.J., what are *you* doing here?" Ryan whispered in my ear right after the picture was finished.

"I jumped down from the other side of the bleachers after the camera took my picture over there," I explained. "Then I ran over here."

"Why did you do that?" asked Michael.

"So I could be in the picture twice!" I told them. "Two heads are better than one!"

"A.J., you're a genius!" said Ryan.

I should get the Nobel Prize for that idea. That's a prize they give out to people who don't have bells.

Fabulo

After Ms. Joni took the school picture, we had to go back to our classroom and wait to be called for our class picture. Mr. Cooper said we could sit at our desks and talk to each other as long as we used our inside voices.

That makes no sense at all. My voice is

the same wherever I am.

I took a sheet of paper from my desk and drew a picture of a rocket ship. Alexia read a book on skateboarding. Andrea and Emily took mirrors out of Andrea's suitcase and started fussing with their hair.

"Maybe Ms. Joni will notice me," Andrea whispered as she put some girly gunk on her face. "It would be exciting to be a model."

Ugh. I really wanted to say something mean about Andrea's face, but it's hard to say mean stuff with an inside voice.

Finally, after we sat there for a million hundred hours, an announcement came over the loudspeaker.

"Attention, Mr. Cooper's class. Please report to the gym to have your class picture taken."

We lined up in size order and walked to the gym. A plain white background was on the wall in the corner, and there were seats in front of it for the class to sit on. Ms. Joni had two big umbrellas set on either side. That was weird.

"Do you think it's going to rain inside the gym?" Ryan asked her.

"No, silly!" said Ms. Joni. "The umbrellas are here to bounce the lights on you and make you look fabulous."

Ms. Joni told us to sit down. There was a sign that said MR. COOPER'S THIRD-GRADE CLASS. We had to sit boy-girl-boy-girl so we couldn't sit next to anybody we liked. Mr. Cooper stood next to the class.

"This is going to be fabulous!" said Ms. Joni. "Are you kids ready?"

"Yes!" said all the girls.

"No!" said all the boys.

Ms. Joni pushed a button, and a big

flash went off. The light bounced off the umbrellas.

Snap!

"That's fabulous!" Ms. Joni said. "Now tilt your heads to the right."

Snap!

"A little to the left."

Snap!

"Chins up."

Snap!

"Not that far. Don't squint."

Snap!

"Keep your cheeks down."

Snap!

"Hands to your sides."

Snap!

"Cross your feet at the ankles."

Snap!

"Look at me."

Snap!

"Now look over my head."

Snap!

"Keep your hands folded in front of you."

Snap!

"Sit perfectly still."

Snap!

"Fabulous!"

Ms. Joni went on like that for a million hundred minutes. Finally, she put the camera down.

"*You* were fabulous!" said Ms. Joni, who

probably says that to everybody. "You can go back to class. We will shoot your personal pictures after all the class photos are done."

We lined up in single file to go back to our classroom. I was just about to walk out the door when the weirdest thing in the history of the world happened. Ms. Joni came running over to me.

"Excuse me," she said. "What is your name, young man?"

"Who? Me?" I asked. "My name is A.J."

"Not anymore," said Ms. Joni. "From now on, your name is . . . Fabulo."

WHAT?!

Ms. Joni was looking at me really weirdly.

"You're *perfect*!" she said, walking around me. "You have the look!"

"Huh?" I asked. "What look?"

Ms. Joni picked up her camera and started snapping pictures of me.

"I've been waiting my whole life to find a young man who looks like you," she said. "And here you are. You are Fabulo! I'm going to make you a star!"

Andrea had on her mean face.

"Star?" I asked. "W-what are you going to do to me?"

"She's gonna make you into a male model, dude," Ryan told me.

"Oh no, not just a model," said Ms. Joni. "Fabulo will be the first male *super*-model!"

"But I don't *want* to be a supermodel!" I told Ms. Joni.

"You were *born* to be Fabulo," she replied as she took more pictures of me. "There's no point in fighting it. Just look at those cheekbones! They're perfect!"

I covered my cheeks with my hands.

"B-but . . . but . . . but . . ."

Everybody was giggling because I said "but," which sounds just like "butt" even though it's missing a "t."

"Dude, being the first male supermodel will probably pay *big* bucks," Michael told me. "And all you have to do is pose for some dumb pictures. This could pay for your college education."

"But I don't *want* to get a college education!" I protested.

"You could build a skate park with the money," Ryan told me, "or a video game arcade. You'll be able to buy whatever you want, man!"

"How much money are we talking about?" I asked.

"Hundreds!" said Michael.

"Thousands!" said Ryan.

"Millions!" said Ms. Joni.

"Bazillions!" said Neil.

I don't even know if bazillions is a real number. We never learned about bazillions in math.

Andrea was standing there the whole time with her arms crossed.

"That's not fair!" she said. "Arlo doesn't even *want* to be a model."

But Ms. Joni wasn't paying any attention to Andrea. She couldn't stop staring at me and taking pictures.

"What do you say?" she asked me. "Do you want to be Fabulo, the first male supermodel, or do you just want to be some plain old boring kid?"

I didn't know what to say. I didn't know what to do. I had to think fast. This was the hardest decision of my life. I could go on being a normal kid, or I could become the first male supermodel in the history of the world. I was concentrating so hard that my brain hurt.

Finally, I decided. I could make bazillions, and I could make Andrea jealous. All I had to do was let Ms. Joni take some dumb pictures of me.

"I'll do it!" I said. "I am Fabulo!"

6

The Vomitorium

It was lunchtime, so we had to go to the vomitorium.

"Welcome to Café LaGrange," said our lunch lady, Ms. LaGrange. "What can I get you for lunch today?"

"I'll have spaghetti with lots of tomato sauce," said Ryan.

"I'll have macaroni and cheese," said Michael.

"I'll have a Sloppy Joe sandwich," said Andrea.

"How about you, A.J.?" said Ms. LaGrange. "Would you like some peas today?"

"No thank you," I told her. "I don't like peas."

"Oh come on," she said. "Give peas a chance."

Then she started singing that dumb song she always sings: *All we are saying is give peas a chance.*

Ms. LaGrange is strange. One time she wrote a secret message in the mashed potatoes.

I looked at the other dishes Ms. LaGrange had prepared. Beef-and-bean burritos. Sloppy Joe sandwiches. Chili Surprise. Chocolate pudding. Pickle chips. Applesauce. Tater Tots.

It all looked disgusting. Luckily, my mom packed a peanut butter and jelly sandwich for me. I just bought a carton

of milk, and we found a table that was empty.

"The guy who thought of putting peanut butter and jelly together was a genius," I told everybody. "That guy should win the Nobel Prize."

"It could have been a *lady*, Arlo," said Andrea, who still had on her mean face.

Andrea was right. A lady could have invented the peanut butter and jelly sandwich. But I wasn't about to admit that Andrea was right about anything.

"I'm so excited that you're going to be the first male supermodel, A.J." said Alexia. "You'll get to walk down a runway and everything!"

"While the planes are taking off?" I asked. "That sounds dangerous."

"Not *that* kind of a runway, dumb-head!" Andrea said, rolling her eyes. "I can't believe you're going to be a super-model, and you don't even know what a runway is."

"You're just being mean to me because you're jealous that Ms. Joni picked *me* to be a supermodel instead of you," I told Andrea.

"I am not jealous!" Andrea shouted.

"Are too!"

"R2-D2!"

"C-3PO!"

We went on like that for a while. Andrea

knew I was right, but she just didn't want to admit it.

"Hey," said Neil. "How about we play football in the playground during recess?"

"Sure," said Ryan.

"Count me in," said Alexia.

"Great idea," said Michael.

"Uh, I'm not in the mood," I said.

Everybody looked at me.

"What's the matter, A.J.?" asked Alexia.

"I just don't want to play football today," I told her.

"But you *love* playing football," Ryan said. "What's the matter, dude?"

"Okay, okay," I admitted. "Ms. Joni is going to be doing a photo shoot with me this afternoon. I don't want to get my hair messed up."

Everybody started laughing, even though I didn't say anything funny.

"Are you kidding, A.J.?" asked Neil. "You're really afraid of messing up your hair?"

"How about we play on the monkey bars instead?" suggested Alexia.

"Yeah!" said Ryan and Michael. "The monkey bars are cool."

"You guys go ahead," I said. "I'll stay in here. If I fell off the monkey bars, I might damage my face. If I broke a cheekbone, my male modeling career would be over."

"Oh come on, A.J.!" said Michael. "You're not going to break a cheekbone."

"Not today, guys," I said. "Sorry."

Now Andrea wasn't the only one who had on a mean face. *Everybody* was looking at me with mean faces.

"You've changed, man," said Ryan. "You're not the same A.J. that I used to know."

"Yeah," said Michael. "Ever since you became the first male supermodel, you're no fun anymore."

"What?!" I said. "I'm not even a supermodel yet!"

"It's only a matter of time," said Alexia. "You're all full of yourself now."

Well, of *course* I was full of myself. I was entirely made up of *me*. I *had* to be full of myself. I couldn't very well be full of somebody *else*.

"I remember the good old days when you were cool, A.J.," said Ryan. "You're not cool anymore."

What!? *Nobody* says I'm not cool. I'm the coolest kid *ever*. It wasn't fair. My best friends had suddenly turned against me. This was the worst thing to happen since TV Turnoff Week.

I felt a sudden rage building up inside. I don't know what came over me. I couldn't control myself. So I did the only thing I could do under the circumstances.

I picked up Ryan's plate of spaghetti and dumped it over his head.

For a second, everybody was in shock. Tomato sauce was dripping down Ryan's ears.

"Oh, snap!" said Ryan.

"You can't do that to my friend!" Michael shouted. Then he took his macaroni and cheese and pushed it into my face.

"There!" he said. "You don't look like a supermodel *now*."

"That wasn't very nice!" said Andrea. She threw her Sloppy Joe sandwich at Michael. But he ducked and it hit Emily instead. She started yelling and screaming and shrieking and hooting and hollering and freaking out, of course.

"Food fight!" somebody shouted.

I'm not exactly sure what happened after that. Things got out of control. The next thing anyone knew, the air was filled with flying food. Some second grader chucked a plate full of Chili Surprise at the kid across the table from him. A beef-and-bean burrito whizzed past my head. Neil got hit in the face with chocolate pudding. It was raining Tater Tots. Pickle chips were flying around.

Somebody took a pepper shaker and started hitting meatballs up in the air like they were baseballs. Kids were squirting ketchup packets at each other. You should have *been* there!*

Eventually, we ran out of food. Café LaGrange was a mess. All four of the basic food groups were stuck to the wall, and to us.

That's when an announcement came over the loudspeaker.

"Happy Picture Day, everyone! Recess has been canceled. We don't want you boys and girls to get dirty before your

*Don't try this at home, kids!

pictures are taken. Mr. Cooper's class, please report to the gym."

"Oh no!" shouted Andrea. "My face is a mess! And my hair is full of applesauce!"

"This is the worst Picture Day *ever*!" said Emily.

Fabulous News!

When our class arrived at the gym, it looked like we had been through a war. Food was dripping off everybody. My hair was all over the place. My shirt was untucked. My new suit was a mess.

My career as the first male supermodel was over, for sure. But it was okay. I didn't really want to be a supermodel anyway.

"What happened?" asked Ms. Joni when she saw us come into the gym.

"There was a food fight in the vomi-torium," whined Andrea. "And now I'm having a bad-hair day. Where's a mirror? I need to fix my hair!"

"Why, is your hair broken?" I asked her.

"That's not funny, Arlo!" Andrea yelled.

"I have a cowlick," complained Michael.

"You licked a cow?" I asked him. "Gross!"

"It's not funny, A.J.!" Michael yelled.

"My pants are full of chocolate pudding!" said Neil.

"Who needs pants?" I told him. "The pictures are from the waist up anyway."

"This is no laughing matter, A.J.!" Neil yelled.

Nobody was in the mood for jokes. Everybody was upset. Well, not everybody. Ms. Joni gathered us all around her.

"Don't worry," she said. "My team of photo flunkies is going to make you all look fabulous."

At that moment, a bunch of ladies came out of the locker room. They were carrying towels and spray bottles and brushes and all kinds of junk with them. They started cleaning everybody up and combing their hair. While they were working on the other kids, Ms. Joni came over and put her arm around me.

"Fabulo, I have fabulous news!" she whispered in my ear. "Remember those pictures I took of you? Well, during lunch I emailed them to *Sports America* magazine, and they want to put you on the cover!"

"WOW," I said, which is "MOM" upside down. "*Sports America*? Cool! My dad reads *Sports America*."

"Yes," said Ms. Joni. "You're going to look fabulous on the cover of the *Sports*

America swimsuit issue!"

WHAT?!

The swimsuit issue? That's the issue of *Sports America* where they have a bunch of models running around in bathing suits! I know, because my dad hides it in the garage.

"B-but . . . but . . . but . . ."

"You're going to be fabulous!" said Ms. Joni, giving me a bathing suit to put on. "I can't wait to shoot pictures of you."

But first, Ms. Joni said she had to take yearbook pictures of all the other kids. Everybody was looking into mirrors and combing their hair.

"Can I go first?" asked Ryan as he put

on his sunglasses. "I want to look like a secret agent."

"Sure!" said Ms. Joni.

She had Ryan stand in front of a big green screen. Then she pushed a button on her computer, and a picture of a racing car appeared on the screen behind Ryan.

It looked just like he was standing in front of the car. It was cool.

Snap!

Ryan slinked around like a secret agent, and Ms. Joni took his picture.

Snap!

"Smile!" she told Ryan.

"Secret agents don't smile," Ryan replied. "Smiling isn't cool."

"Oh, yeah?" said Ms. Joni. "Then I'll tell you a joke to make you smile."

"It won't work," Ryan said. "Nobody can make me smile if I don't want to."

"What's brown and sticky?" asked Ms. Joni.

"What?"

"A brown stick!" said Ms. Joni.

That was totally not funny. Ryan didn't laugh.

"Okay," said Ms. Joni, "you have forced me to say the *one* word in the English language that's guaranteed to make any third grader laugh."

Everybody leaned forward. We wanted to know the one word in the English language that would make us laugh. We were all on pins and needles.

Well, not really. We were just standing there. If we were on pins and needles, it would have hurt.

"What word is it?" I asked.

"Do you *really* want me to say it?" asked

Ms. Joni. "It's naughty."

"Yes!" we all shouted.

"Okay," said Ms. Joni. "Here it is. The word is . . . 'UNDERWEAR'!"

Ryan cracked up, and Ms. Joni took the picture.

Snap!

She was right. We all cracked up when she said the word "underwear." It's the one word in the English language that's guaranteed to make any third grader laugh. Nobody knows why.

Ms. Joni let everybody pick costumes and props out of a big box and then had them stand in front of the green screen. She could project just about any background on it. Michael stood in front of the White House holding a soccer ball. Neil stood on a mountaintop with a sombrero on his head. Andrea stood in the middle of a forest holding a teddy bear. Everybody's picture looked different. It was cool.

"Fabulous!" said Ms Joni. "I think we're just about finished with your class. There's just one more student I need to shoot. . . . Fabulo!"

Photobomb

I came out of the locker room wearing the bathing suit Ms. Joni had given me, and everybody went nuts. They were all whistling and hooting and hollering.

"Do I *really* have to wear this?" I asked.

"You look fabulous, Fabulo!" said Ms. Joni.

"And remember," said Ryan, "you're going to make bazillions."

A bunch of Ms. Joni's flunkies swarmed all over me. They put some stinky gunk on my hair, and then they combed and blow-dried it. It looked weird. Ms. Joni gave me a surfboard and told me to stand in front of the green screen.

She pushed a button, and a picture of the ocean appeared on the screen so it looked like I was standing on the beach. Next, she turned on bright lights and a big fan, and pointed them at me. I was blinded, and my hair was blowing all over the place.

"This will make it look like you're on

a windswept tropical paradise," Ms. Joni said as she picked up her camera. "They love that at *Sports America*. Okay, let's make some magic, people!"

"What should I do?" I asked.

"Just be your fabulous self, Fabulo," she replied.

I moved a garbage can to the front of

the screen and put the surfboard on top of it. Then I climbed up and pretended to be surfing. Ms. Joni took the picture.

Snap!

"Fabulous!" shouted Ms. Joni. "Now drop your chin, Fabulo."

"I can't drop my chin," I told her. "It's attached to my head. How am I supposed to drop it?"

"Leg up," shouted Ms. Joni.

I put my leg up.

Snap!

"Not there. *There.*"

Snap!

"That's fabulous! Tilt your head to the right."

Snap!

"No, a little left."

Snap!

"Smile."

Snap!

"Now frown."

Snap!

"Put the surfboard on your head."

Snap!

"Look like you just tasted ice cream for the first time."

Snap!

"Now look like you just ate some food that's past its expiration date."

Snap!

"Look like you just found out there's no school tomorrow."

Snap!

"Look like your dog just died."

Snap!

"Fabulous! The camera loves you! You're an *animal,* Fabulo! Pretend to be a tiger."

"I thought you just wanted me to be myself," I said.

"Be yourself," said Ms. Joni, "but with more teeth."

Snap!

"A little *more* teeth."

"These are all the

teeth I have!" I yelled.

Snap!

It went on like that for a million hundred minutes. I was exhausted. But it would be worth it to be a famous supermodel making bazillions.

That's when the strangest thing in the history of the world happened. Ms. Joni put down the camera. It looked like something was wrong.

"What's *that*?" she said, pointing behind me.

I turned around.

Out of the corner of my eye, I spotted something. Or somebody. There was movement.

It was big.

It was hairy.

It was scary.

And it was running away.

It could have been Bigfoot. It could have been an alien from another planet. It could have been *anything*.

Everybody started shouting and pointing.

"It's a monster!" shouted Ryan.

"It's a zombie!" shouted Neil.

"It's the Picture Day Zombie!" I shouted.

Chase Scenes
Are Cool

"Run for your lives!" shouted Neil the nude kid.

Okay, I *know* I told you there weren't going to be any zombies in this book. But what am I supposed to do? Zombies don't tell you when they're coming. The Picture Day Zombie just showed up! I have no control over what zombies do in their spare time.

"Grab that zombie!" I shouted.

It was too late. The zombie had already dashed out of the gym.

"Get him!" Ryan shouted.

My whole class ran out of the gym and down the hall just in time to see the zombie turn the corner.

"That zombie is *fast*!" shouted Alexia.

We chased the zombie past the science room.

Past the all-purpose room.

Past the front office.

Mr. Klutz was standing there.

"No running in the halls, kids!" he

shouted at us.

"We're chasing a zombie!" I shouted to him.

"Oh, then running is okay," shouted Mr. Klutz.

We were gaining on the zombie, but then it ran out the back door of the school into the playground.

"Grab it before it escapes into the woods!" shouted Michael.

Isn't this exciting? Chase scenes are always exciting. They should have a TV channel that shows nothing but chase scenes. I would watch that all day.

Anyway, we chased the zombie past the monkey bars and the soccer field. Finally, we caught up with it at the edge of the playground.

We tackled it and pinned it to the ground.

The zombie tried to get free, but we wouldn't let go.

It had a hideous face. I thought I was gonna throw up. But then I realized that the zombie's hideous face was actually some kind of hideous rubber mask.

"It's time to reveal the true identity of the Picture Day Zombie!" I announced.

Carefully, I lifted the hideous mask off the zombie's head. And you'll never believe whose face was underneath.

I could make you wait until the next chapter to find out who the zombie was.

But that would be mean.

I could tell you that we were all on pins and needles.

But that would be mean.

I could say there was electricity in the air.

But that would be mean.

I could say we were glued to our seats.

But that would be mean. And weird. Who puts glue on seats?

So I'll just tell you. The Picture Day Zombie was . . . Andrea!*

---

*Betcha didn't see *that* coming! The Picture Day Zombie wasn't a zombie after all. So I guess you can still say there are no zombies in this book.

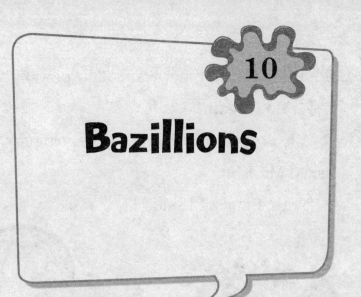

Bazillions

"Eeeek!" screamed Emily. "Andrea! *You're* the Picture Day Zombie? How could you do such a thing?"

Everybody was out in the playground now, even Mr. Klutz. Andrea was crying.

"I was mad because Arlo is going to be a supermodel instead of me," Andrea admitted through her tears. "I'm sorry. I'll never do it again."

"A.J., do you accept Andrea's apology?" asked Mr. Klutz.

"Yeah, I guess," I said.

"*Ooooo!*" Ryan said. "A.J. accepted Andrea's apology. They must be in *love!*"

"When are you gonna get married?" asked Michael.

If those guys weren't my best friends, I would hate them.

When we got back inside the school, Ms. Joni had left. I figured she went to *Sports America* to give them the pictures of me. It was only a matter of time until I would be a famous supermodel earning bazillions.

But that didn't happen. A week went by and I didn't hear from Ms. Joni. I was beginning to think that Ms. Joni was a phony.

But then, a couple of days later, I was in Mr. Cooper's class when an announcement came over the loudspeaker.

"A.J., please report to Mr. Klutz's office."

"Ooooo!" Ryan said. "A.J. is in trouble!"

I walked by myself to Mr. Klutz's office. I figured he was going to tell me that I would have to leave school to go become a famous supermodel. Instead of learning math and stuff, I would be spending all my time traveling around the world on photo shoots and dancing at discos with other supermodels.

But that didn't happen either. You'll never believe who was in the office with Mr. Klutz.

Ms. Joni!

"Hello, A.J.," she said.

"A.J.?" I replied. "My name is Fabulo, remember?"

"Not anymore," Ms. Joni told me. "Those

pictures I took of you were ruined by the fake zombie. So you're not going to be in the *Sports America* swimsuit issue after all. I'm sorry."

Bummer in the summer!

"But that's not why I called you down here, A.J.," said Mr. Klutz as he opened his drawer. "The school yearbook is in."

"Cool!" I said. "Can I see it?"

Mr. Klutz took out the yearbook and turned to the photo of the whole school.

"Can you explain this, A.J.?" Mr. Klutz asked me.

"Explain what?"

"I see your face on *this* side of the photo," he said, pointing to the picture, "and then

I see your face again on the *other* side of the photo."

I didn't know what to say. I didn't know what to do. I had to think fast.

"Uh . . . one of those two guys isn't me," I finally said. "That's my twin brother. His name is . . . P.J."

"P.J.?" said Mr. Klutz. "I didn't know you had a twin brother."

"Oh, yeah," I told him. "P.J. was just visiting that day. He lives in . . . Antarctica."

"Why does your twin brother live in Antarctica?" asked Ms. Joni.

"He . . . uh . . . lives with a family of penguins," I explained.

"Um-hmm," said Mr. Klutz. "So when will we get to meet this twin brother of yours?"

"He, uh, went back to Antarctica," I explained. "The penguins were hungry."

"I see," Mr. Klutz said.

I think he believed my story. He gave me the yearbook and said I could go back to class.

Out in the hallway, I flipped through the yearbook to see what my surfing picture looked like. I found the page with my

name on it. And you'll never believe in a
million hundred years what it said above
my name.

NO PHOTO
AVAILABLE

WHAT?!

Oh, yeah. I guess I forgot to turn in my
Picture Day money. The envelope was still
in my backpack.

* * *

That's pretty much what happened. Maybe Ms. Joni will stop saying "fabulous" all the time. Maybe that family of zombies will get out of our vacuum cleaner. Maybe the girls will start coming to school with laundry bags over their heads. Maybe we'll have to try on bananas before we buy them. Maybe my mom will blow her nose into her purse. Maybe Ryan will stop wearing diapers. Maybe Emily will rob a bank and go skiing. Maybe supermodels will use their superheat vision to warm up their food. Maybe I'll have my cheekbones removed. Maybe I'll get to walk down a runway while the planes are taking off.

Maybe I'll figure out a way to explain why my twin brother lives in Antarctica with the penguins.

But it won't be easy!*

---

*If you liked this book, tell your friends. If you didn't like it, don't tell anybody.

Dan Gutman

has written many weird books for kids. He lives with his weird wife in New York (a very weird place).

Jim Paillot

lives in Arizona (another weird place) with his weird wife and two weird children. Isn't that weird?